For my family, who cheered me on every step of my journey to write this book.
And to all the changemakers—thank you for being brave.
—T.H.

To my grandparents and parents, who crossed an ocean so that I could go to school
—M.J.C.

Mamie Tape Fights to go to School

BASED ON A TRUE STORY

WRITTEN BY TRACI HUAHN • ILLUSTRATED BY MICHELLE JING CHAN

Crown Books for Young Readers New York

Mamma always said, *A journey of a thousand miles begins with a single step.*

I never thought I could be as brave as her and Papa, each coming from China to begin new lives in America.

But the day I showed up at Spring Valley Primary School, I took my own brave step.

San Francisco didn't allow Chinese children in its schools.

Mamma and I went anyway.

Though we were the only Chinese family in our neighborhood,
my brother and sister and I always played with the other children—

roller-skating . . .

skipping rope . . .

Before I could reach the door, the principal stopped me.
"Your kind is not welcome here."
It felt like the ground had slipped out from under me,
just like my first time roller-skating.
Mamma said to pay no mind. We'd fight it.
But I couldn't forget those words.

Then I remembered, *A journey of a thousand miles begins with a single step.*
My journey was just beginning.

Next step. We asked the school superintendent to let me in.
Papa said there used to be a separate school for Chinese children in
the bottom of a church basement. To keep us away from white children.

The school board closed it years before I was
born. To stop us from going to school at all.
Though many tried.

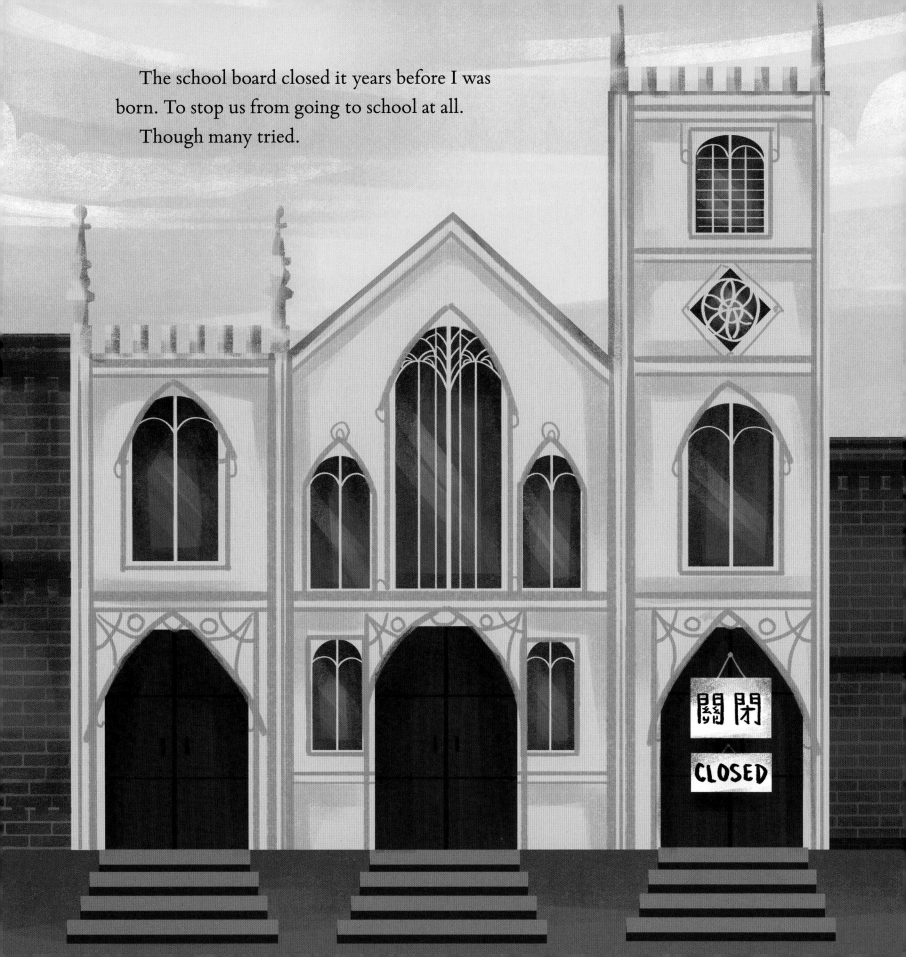

Like a white reverend who preached to admit a Chinese boy. Some folks got so angry they threw rocks at the reverend's home, broke the windows.

Or the Chinese merchants who demanded schools for thousands of Chinese children.
Papa said most Americans didn't want Chinese people working here, settling down,
and raising children who would need to go to school.
So the answer was always no.

The school superintendent told me no, too.
I wanted to throw rocks at his windows.
Instead, we took *another step*. We hired two
lawyers to fight for me.

One of my lawyers told a judge the law gave me the right to go to school.

I waited to hear if he'd agree. Some days the journey really seemed a thousand miles.

Mornings, my neighbor tutored me. I read books and practiced arithmetic. I didn't understand why some folks thought Chinese children couldn't be taught.

Afternoons, I played with friends, reciting their schoolyard rhymes by heart. Sometimes I imagined myself skipping rope at school.

I like coffee,
I like tea,
I like Mamie to jump with me.
One, two, three . . .

Finally, we heard: the judge agreed!

Daily Alta California.

SAN FRANCISCO, SATURDAY MORNING, JANUARY 10, 1885

CHINESE IN OUR SCHOOLS.

Judge Maguire Says They Have Same Rights as Others.

CONTRIBUTIONS BY FORCE.

The Court Holds That it Has No Power to Avert a Danger Which Springs From the Absence of Necessary Laws—Right of Appeal.

The case of Mamie Tape vs. Miss Jennie M. A. Hurley et al., a petition for a writ of mandate to compel the members of the Board of Education, Superintendent of Schools and Principal Teacher of the Spring Valley Primary School as a pupil, was decided yesterday by Judge Maguire. It is alleged in the petition that Mamie Tape, (a Chinese child), is eight years of age, a native of California, in good health, good character and cleanly habits; that her parents are residents of this city and county; that her father, Joseph Tape, is and has been for many years a householder and taxpayer; has applied for admission to the Spring Valley Primary School, and that although there was room for her accommodation the petition solely because she

THE MOTION DENIED.

Judge Maguire, in his decision, denied the motion of respondent to quash the alternative writ of mandate and overrules the demurrer, and in the course of his decision says: "The only reason urged against Mamie Tape's admission is that she, in common with other Chinese born children, is descended from the Mongolian race, she is a Chinese born and is participating in the benefits of the public education, which are for the children of all other races—white, black and copper-colored. There is no law which is susceptible of such construction; and if there were, it would be void, as being in direct conflict with the Fourteenth Amendment to the Constitution of the United States, which provides that all persons naturalized in the United States and subject to the jurisdiction thereof, are citizens of the United States and of the State in which they reside, and that no State shall make or enforce any law which shall abridge the privileges or immunities of citizens of the United States, nor shall any State deprive any person of life, liberty or property, without due process of law; nor deny to any person within its jurisdiction the equal protection of the laws.

... having thus established ... it is not necessary in this decision to inquire ... of our State laws ... but as I conceive ... necessary upon our ... if it should ... taxes were levied for ... of special taxes ... etc. ... Political ... Chinese residents, ... to in the benefits ... levied. The right ... to be educated for ... seems to have ... legislature. For

But still no school. The school board fought back. That meant *another step*.
I waited for California's most powerful court to have the final say.

It felt like two steps forward, one step back.

Everyone knew about my case. Newspapers plastered my name on front
pages, next to words like *heathen, barbarian, trouble,* and *disaster.* I wasn't sure
what all those meant, just that they weren't good. If only folks who believed
those stories knew me like my friends did.

The year of the rooster arrived. Lanterns and spring couplets
adorned Chinatown's streets. Mamma rarely shopped there
except to buy foods like lily buds, fat choy, and bamboo shoots.

For Chinese New Year, we always cooked jai to welcome good luck.
Maybe that would help me get into school. I slurped up an extra helping.

The lucky jai worked! The court said I could go to school.
Lawyers by my side, I walked up to the schoolhouse.
The principal declared, "You must have a vaccination
certificate. From a doctor who's not Chinese."
I felt like I'd fallen a hundred steps back.

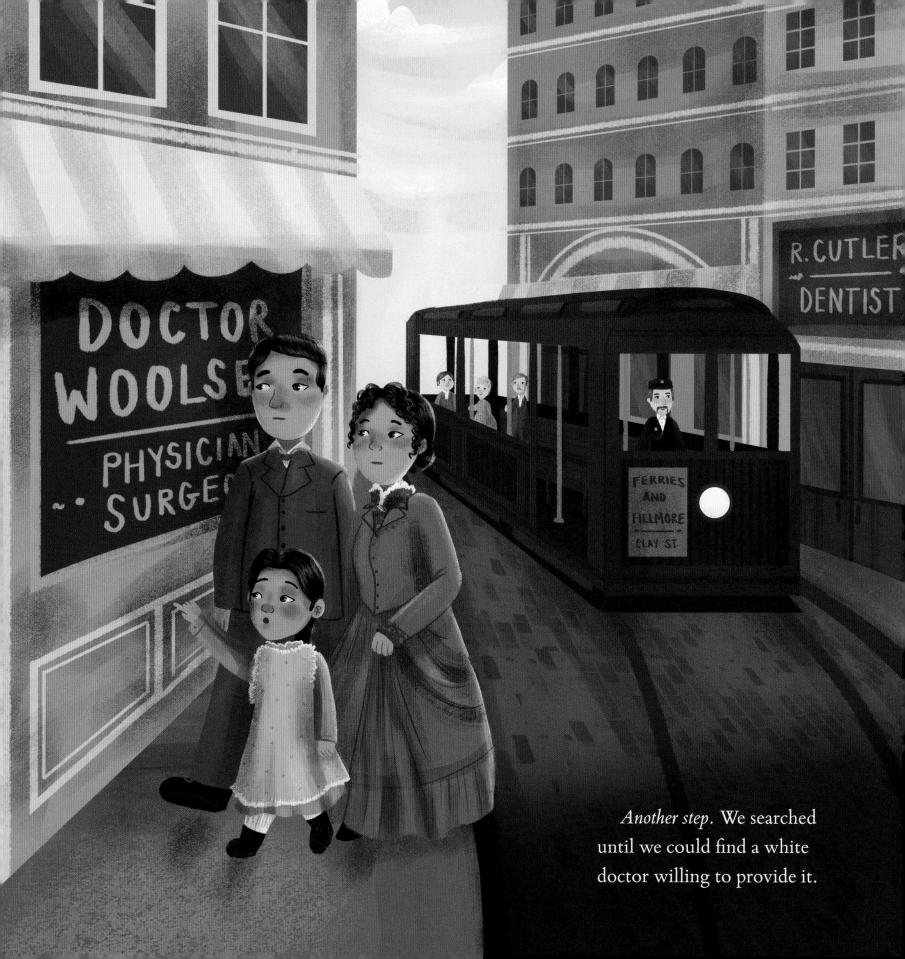

Another step. We searched until we could find a white doctor willing to provide it.

Next day, fingers crossed, it would be my first day of school.

Without looking at my vaccination certificate, the principal scoffed, "There's no room for you here. No more than sixty pupils are allowed."

Yet the classes for eight-year-olds had sixty-two and seventy white children.

The principal said I could wait for a spot to open up.

I didn't think one ever would.

I felt like I'd tumbled a thousand steps back.

The school board announced they were opening a separate school for Chinese children. Again.

My lawyers explained I won the right to go to school, but the school board still had the right to keep Chinese children segregated. I'd have to go to that school.

Across town.

Above a grocery store.

With no play yard.

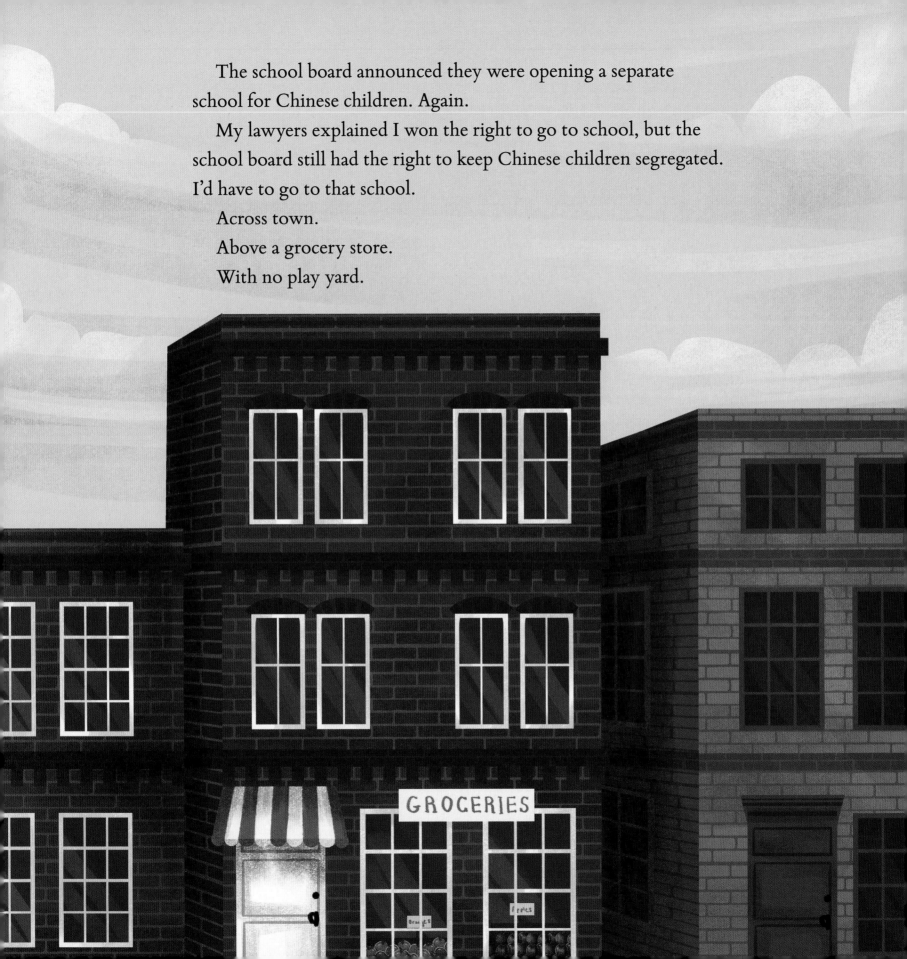

There were no more steps.
I curled up in my favorite hide-and-seek spot,
hoping I'd never be found.
Papa shouted words I'd never heard.
Mamma vowed never to send me there.

Later, I thought about all those years Chinese children couldn't go to school at all.
Because of the steps I'd taken, there was now one public school where we were welcome.
This time, no one could shut it down.

I reminded Mamma, *A journey of a thousand miles begins with a single step*.
Maybe the journey wasn't over, and this was just one small step in the right direction.
I told her and Papa I still wanted to go to school.

The day the Chinese school opened, I walked up to the classroom. I was the first pupil to step through the door.

EPILOGUE TO THE CHINESE PRIMARY SCHOOL

The Chinese Primary School opened on April 13, 1885. Mamie and her younger brother, Frank, were the first students to attend.

In 1906, the school was renamed the Oriental School, and the San Francisco Board of Education issued a policy requiring all children of Chinese, Japanese, and Korean heritage to attend that school. After California outlawed racially segregated schools in 1947, that policy was no longer enforced. However, it was not officially removed from the San Francisco Unified School District's policies until seventy years later, on January 24, 2017.

Chinese Primary School, c. 1890. Mamie (center, second row) and her brother, Frank (far right, second row), with classmates.

AUTHOR'S NOTE

Tape family, 1884, taken around the time of Mamie's case.
Left to right: Joseph, Emily, Mamie, Frank, and Mary.

Mamie Tape and the Long Fight for Equality

Mamie Tape Fights to Go to School is inspired by the real-life story of eight-year-old Mamie Tape and her 1885 California Supreme Court case, *Tape v. Hurley.*

Though Mamie's case might not have felt like a victory to her and her family, it was historic for affirming that all children, including those of Chinese heritage, had the right to a free public school education in California, even if still at segregated facilities. Fourteen years prior, the San Francisco school board began excluding Chinese children from its schools by closing its only segregated Chinese school and banning them from neighborhood schools.

In September 1884, when Mamie's parents, Joseph and Mary Tape, sent her to Spring Valley Primary School, they knew Chinese children weren't allowed. Because the Tapes had assimilated into an all-white neighborhood, spoke English at home, and wore American fashions and hairstyles, they thought Mamie would be treated like the white children who were her playmates.

After the ruling, the school board was ordered to admit Mamie to the all-white primary school because there was no separate school for Chinese children. But by delaying Mamie's entry, the school board had enough time to reestablish a new Chinese primary school, leaving Mamie little choice but to go there. Outraged by these underhanded tactics, Mary Tape wrote a powerful letter, printed in newspapers nationwide, that stated in part, "What right! have you to bar my child out of the school because she is a chinese Descend. . . . It seems no matter how a Chinese may live and dress so long as you know they Chinese. Then they are hated as one. There is not any right or justice for them."

The journey to end racially segregated schools really seemed a thousand miles long. It wasn't until 1947, when Mamie was seventy-one years old, that California outlawed racially segregated schools after a case involving eight-year-old Sylvia Mendez, who was Mexican American. In *Mendez v. Westminster,* the court ruled that separate schools for Mexican children were inferior to all-white schools and violated the U.S. Constitution's Equal Protection Clause. Soon after, California's governor signed a law outlawing racially segregated schools throughout the state.

In 1954, racially segregated schools were finally ruled unconstitutional for the entire country in the landmark U.S. Supreme Court case *Brown v. Board of Education*. That case originated with yet another eight-year-old, Linda Brown, who was African American. In a unanimous decision, the U.S. Supreme Court declared, "We conclude that in the field of public education the doctrine of 'separate but equal' has no place. Separate educational facilities are inherently unequal."

Joseph and Mary Tape's Brave Steps

When Mamie's parents filed their lawsuit, it marked the first time anyone had legally challenged the San Francisco school board's policies prohibiting Chinese children in its schools. Because of their courage and relative privilege as a middle-class family, Joseph and Mary were able to fight for Mamie's rights. But their lives didn't start that way.

Both emigrated from China as children with no family and little money. Joseph arrived in 1864 at age twelve, and Mary in 1868 at age eleven. As a boy, Joseph worked as a house servant and later a milk wagon driver. As a girl, Mary found refuge with a women's home that cared for orphaned children. In their new lives, Joseph and Mary learned English and adapted to American ways. Joseph cut off his queue, the braided hairstyle traditionally worn by Chinese men, and changed his name from Jeu Dip to Joseph Tape. In 1875, Joseph and Mary met and married. Mamie was born the next year.

Joseph later built his own successful wagon service, transporting baggage for Chinese laborers, and worked as an interpreter for the Chinese consulate. He became an avid bird hunter, with two hunting dogs, and he

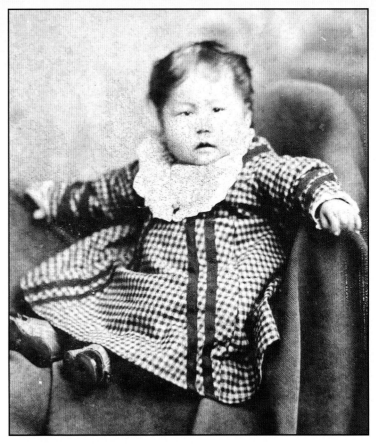

Mamie Tape, 1877

displayed his large collection of stuffed preserved birds in their home. Mary became an accomplished painter and photographer who won local awards. Some of the illustrations in this book were inspired by Joseph's bird collection and Mary's wall art and hand-painted dishes.

When Joseph and Mary sent Mamie to Spring Valley Primary School, it was a brave step not only for going against school rules but for going against Chinese tradition, which at that time didn't believe in educating girls. In her only known interview, Mamie stated that her dad wanted her to go to school just like other Americans. Only his name appears on the legal papers filed in Mamie's case, but Mary Tape's letter shows that she was also a formidable advocate for Mamie.

Author's Steps

This book is historical fiction. Some details, including the dialogue, are imagined, but all the steps that Mamie and those before her took to fight to go to school, and all the ways others tried to stop them, are true.

Because little is known about Mamie's experience of these historic events, I imagined certain details from what is known. For example, the Chinese New Year scene is based on two different memories. According to Mamie's eldest great-granddaughter, Linda Lum Doler, in Mamie's later life she celebrated Chinese New Year by helping to prepare jai, a vegetable dish traditionally served on the first day of the new year. Mamie's mom might have cooked jai, since food was one of the few Chinese traditions the Tape family retained. Mamie recalled that growing up, her family received home deliveries of Chinese vegetables like bok choy and gai lan.

In this book I use the term *Chinese* rather than *Chinese American* because that term wasn't in common use at the time of Mamie's case. I also use a less familiar spelling of the word *mama*. In Mamie's time it was spelled with two *m*'s but is pronounced the same.

A journey of a thousand miles begins with a single step originates from a Chinese proverb most commonly attributed to philosopher Laozi between the fourth and sixth centuries BCE. To me, it poignantly sums up not only Mamie's journey but that of countless others who have fought for and continue to fight for equality.

My research for this book was also a journey of sorts. My first step was learning about *Tape v. Hurley*. I paged through original legal documents; read books, journals, and government reports; pored over historic photos; and read dozens of newspaper articles chronicling Mamie's

Mamie Tape, 1957, at age eighty-one, only a few years after racially segregated schools were finally deemed unconstitutional.

case. I interviewed several of Mamie's living relatives and listened to a recorded interview with Mamie at age ninety-six, conducted by historian Him Mark Lai. To put myself in Mamie's shoes, I visited the address where the Tape family home stood, the former site of Spring Valley Primary School, and the alley where the separate Chinese school once was. Each step of the way, I grew more inspired to tell Mamie's story.

Special thanks to Linda Lum Doler for generously sharing her family's history and photos. And to Alisa J. Kim, great-grandniece of Mamie's brother, Frank, and his wife, Ruby, for providing the Tape family portrait.

Please visit tracihuahn.com for a complete bibliography and free educator guide.

SELECTED BIBLIOGRAPHY

LEGAL SOURCES

A Petition for Separate Chinese Schools, 1878, Digital History, ID 23, digitalhistory.uh.edu.

Tape v. Hurley, 66 Cal. 473 (1885).

Transcript on Appeal, Mamie Tape (an infant) by her Guardian ad litem, Joseph Tape, Respondent, v. Miss Jennie M.A. Hurley, et als., Appellants, In the Supreme Court of the State of California (February 5, 1885).

INTERVIEWS

Doler, Linda Lum, great-granddaughter of Mamie Tape, in discussion with the author, March 3, 2021, March 12, 2021, and March 22, 2021 (via Zoom video conference) and on August 11, 2021 (in person in Portland, Oregon).

Lowe, Mamie Tape, and Emily Lowe Lum, interviewed by Him Mark Lai and Philip Choy, July 29, 1972, Portland, Oregon. (Digitized tape recording, courtesy of Mae Ngai.)

BOOKS

Low, Victor. *The Unimpressible Race: A Century of Educational Struggle by the Chinese in San Francisco.* San Francisco: East/West Publishing Company, 1982.

Ngai, Mae. *The Lucky Ones: One Family and the Extraordinary Invention of Chinese America.* New York: Houghton Mifflin Harcourt, 2010.

PERIODICALS

"A Chinese School. Opening of the First Public School for the Education of Chinese—Six Pupils Appear on the First Day—Bright Scholars Who Fancy Roller Skates." *San Francisco Bulletin,* April 14, 1885.

"A Novel Case. A Chinese Girl Refused Admission to the Public Schools." *San Francisco Examiner,* September 16, 1884.

"Board of Education. A Long and Wordy Session Held Last Evening. Chinese Question Again. The Board Refuses to Listen to Petitions for Admitting Native-Born Chinese Children to the Public Schools." *Daily Alta California,* October 22, 1884.

"Board of Education: A Long Session Indulged in Last Night. Chinese Mother's Letter. The Principal of the Commercial High School Granted a Long Leave of Absence—A Financial Report." *Daily Alta California,* April 16, 1885.

"Board of Education. A Very Long Session Held Last Evening. An Old Teacher Removed. Strong Anti-Chinese Speech Delivered by Director Culver—Bills Ordered Paid Without the Finance Committee's Sanction." *Daily Alta California,* April 2, 1885.

"Board of Education. Special Meeting Held on the Chinese School. Mamie Tape Outwitted. She Attempts to Force Her Way into the Spring Valley School, But Has to Retire, Having No Vaccination Certificate." *Daily Alta California,* April 8, 1885.

"Chinese and the Schools. Writ of Mandate Presented To-day to the Principal of the Spring Valley School." *San Francisco Bulletin,* April 7, 1885.

"Chinese in Our Schools. Judge Maguire Says They Have Same Rights as Others. Contributions by Force. The Court Holds That It Has No Power to Avert a Danger Which Springs From the Absence of Necessary Laws–Right of Appeal." *Daily Alta California,* January 10, 1885.

"Chinese in the Schools: Their Right to Admission Judicially Declared." *San Francisco Chronicle,* January 10, 1885.

"Chinese Schools: One Ordered Established by the Board of Education. Made as Expensive as Possible. The Manner in which Superintendent Moulder Circumvented Mamie Tape's Lawyers." *San Francisco Examiner,* April 8, 1885.

Gamble, Leland. "What a Chinese Girl Did. An Expert Photographer and Telegrapher." *San Francisco Morning Call,* November 23, 1892.

"Mongolian Children: Shall They Be Admitted to Our Public Schools? The Question Discussed by the State Superintendent of Public Instruction." *Sacramento Daily Union,* January 16, 1885.

"Must Admit Her. Judge Maguire Decides the Mamie Tape Case. The Mongol Girl Victorious. Chinese Children Born in the United States Are Entitled to Admission to the Public Schools." *San Francisco Examiner,* January 10, 1885.

"San Francisco Items." *Sacramento Daily Union,* April 15, 1885.

"The Chinese Class. The Two Tape Children Alone Enter the School." *San Francisco Examiner,* April 14, 1885.

"The Chinese School. Opened Yesterday With an Attendance of Six Children." *Daily Alta California,* April 14, 1885.

"The Chinese School. To be Formally Opened on Next Monday— The Tape Girl Not to Attend." *Daily Alta California,* April 10, 1885.

"The Chinese School Problem. Prompt Action Taken in the Legislature to Provide Separate Schools." *Daily Alta California,* March 5, 1885.

"The Tape Case: Expedients Which May Be Resorted to to Avoid Its Consequences." *San Francisco Examiner,* January 16, 1885.

WEBSITES

"SF Board of Education rescinds 1906 resolution that excluded Asians from 'normal' schools." San Francisco Unified School District (website), January 25, 2017.